HERGÉ
★
THE ADVENTURES OF
TINTIN
★
THE
BLACK
ISLAND

 LITTLE, BROWN AND COMPANY
New York ❧ Boston

Little, Brown and Company

Hachette Book Group
237 Park Avenue, New York, NY 10017
Visit our website at www.lb-kids.com

Little, Brown and Company is a division of Hachette Book Group, Inc.
The Little, Brown name and logo are trademarks of Hachette Book Group, Inc.

First U.S. edition: April 1975
ISBN: 978-0-316-35835-4

Library of Congress card catalog no. 74-21624
30 29 28 27 26

Published pursuant to agreement with Casterman, Belgium.
Not for sale in the British Commonwealth.

Printed in China

THE BLACK ISLAND

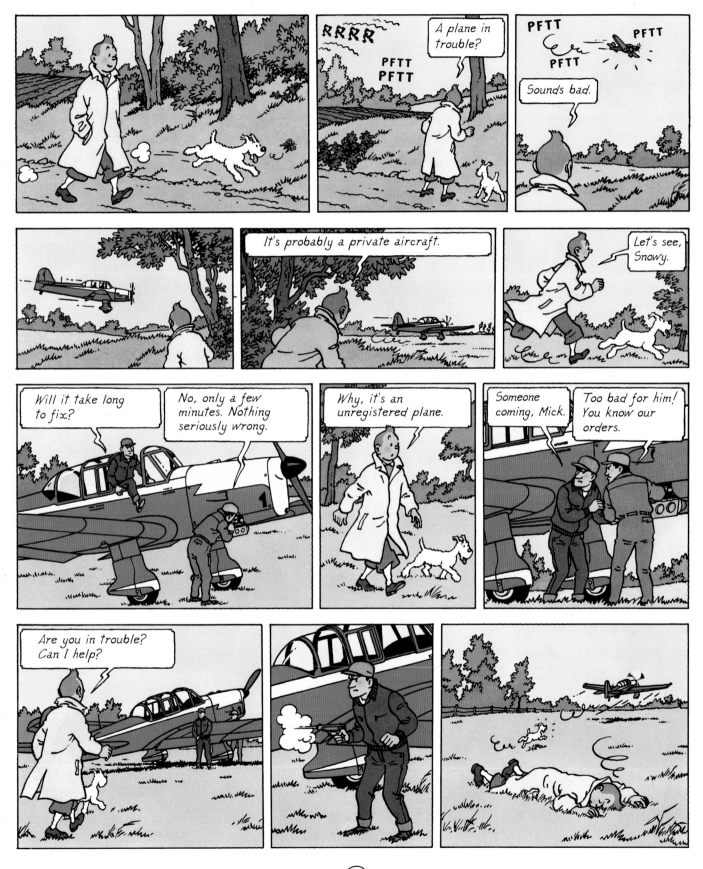

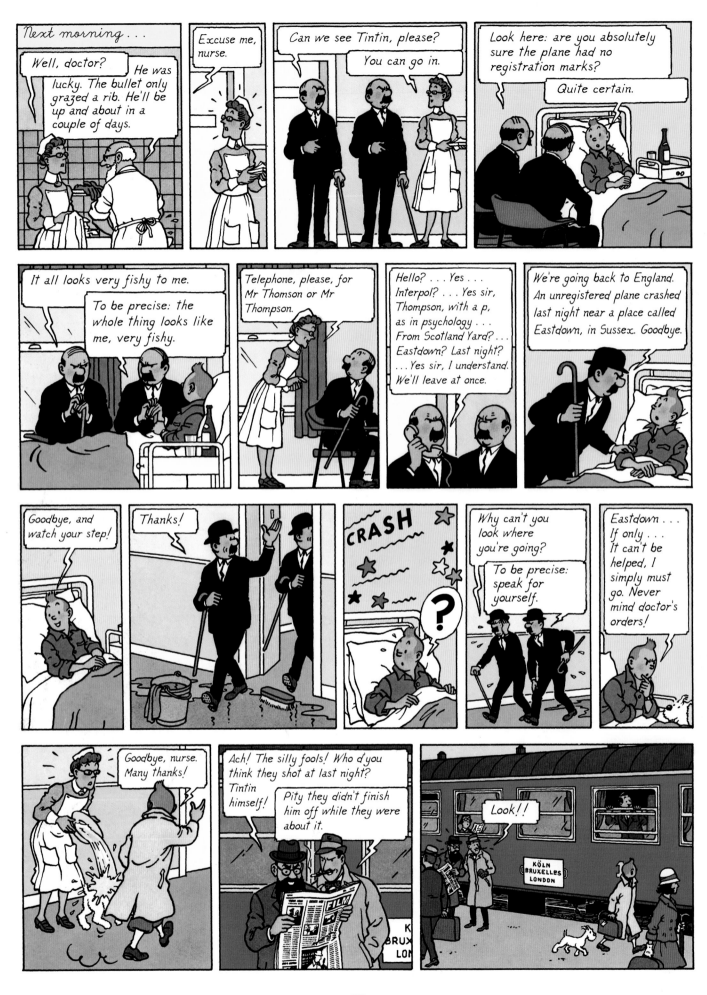

4

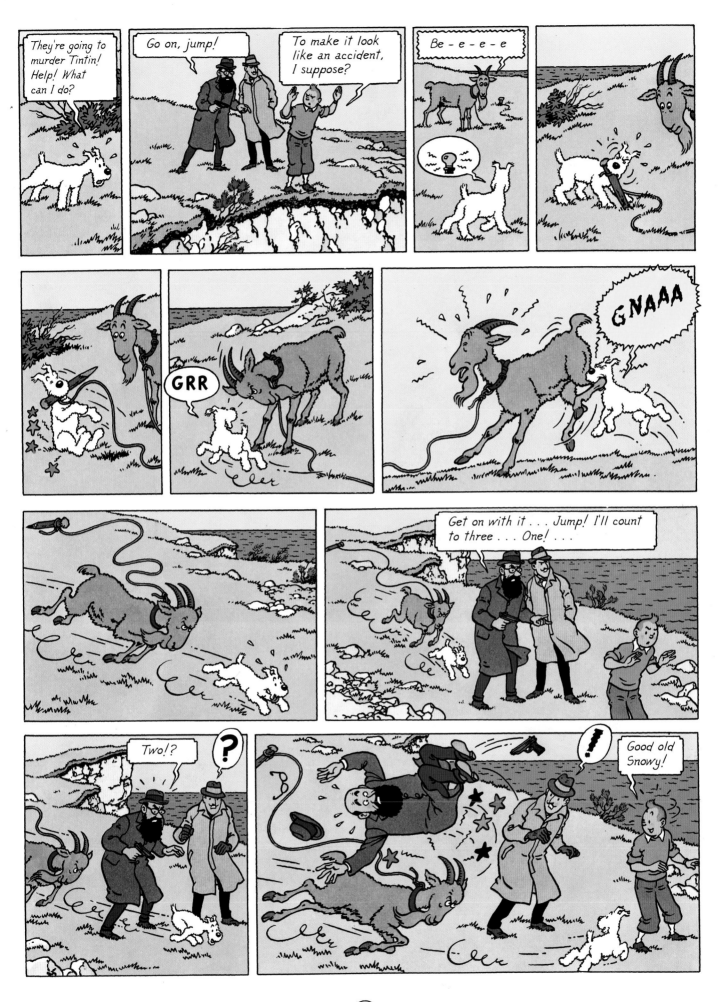

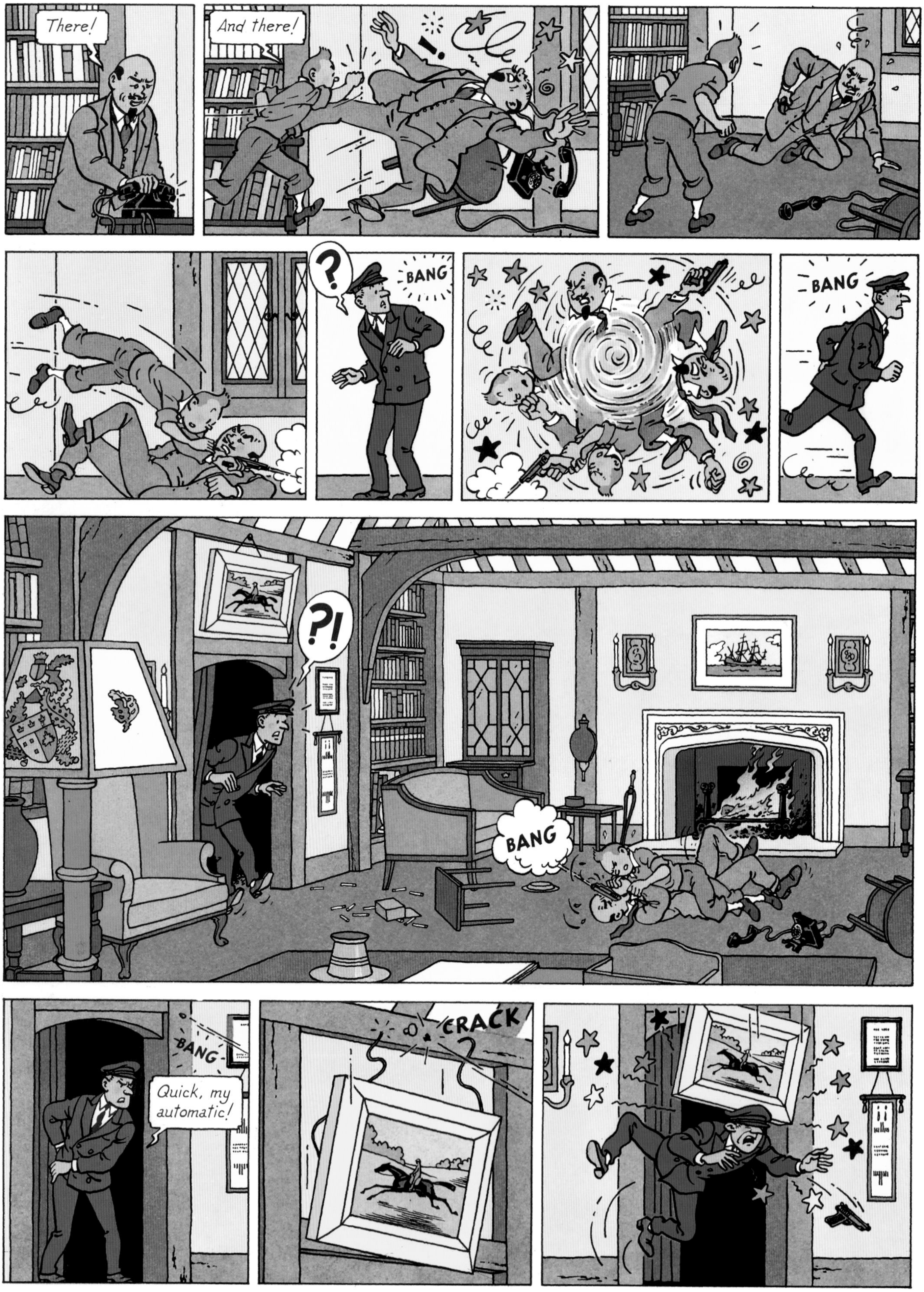

There!
And there!
!
?
BANG
BANG
?!
BANG
BANG
Quick, my automatic!
CRACK

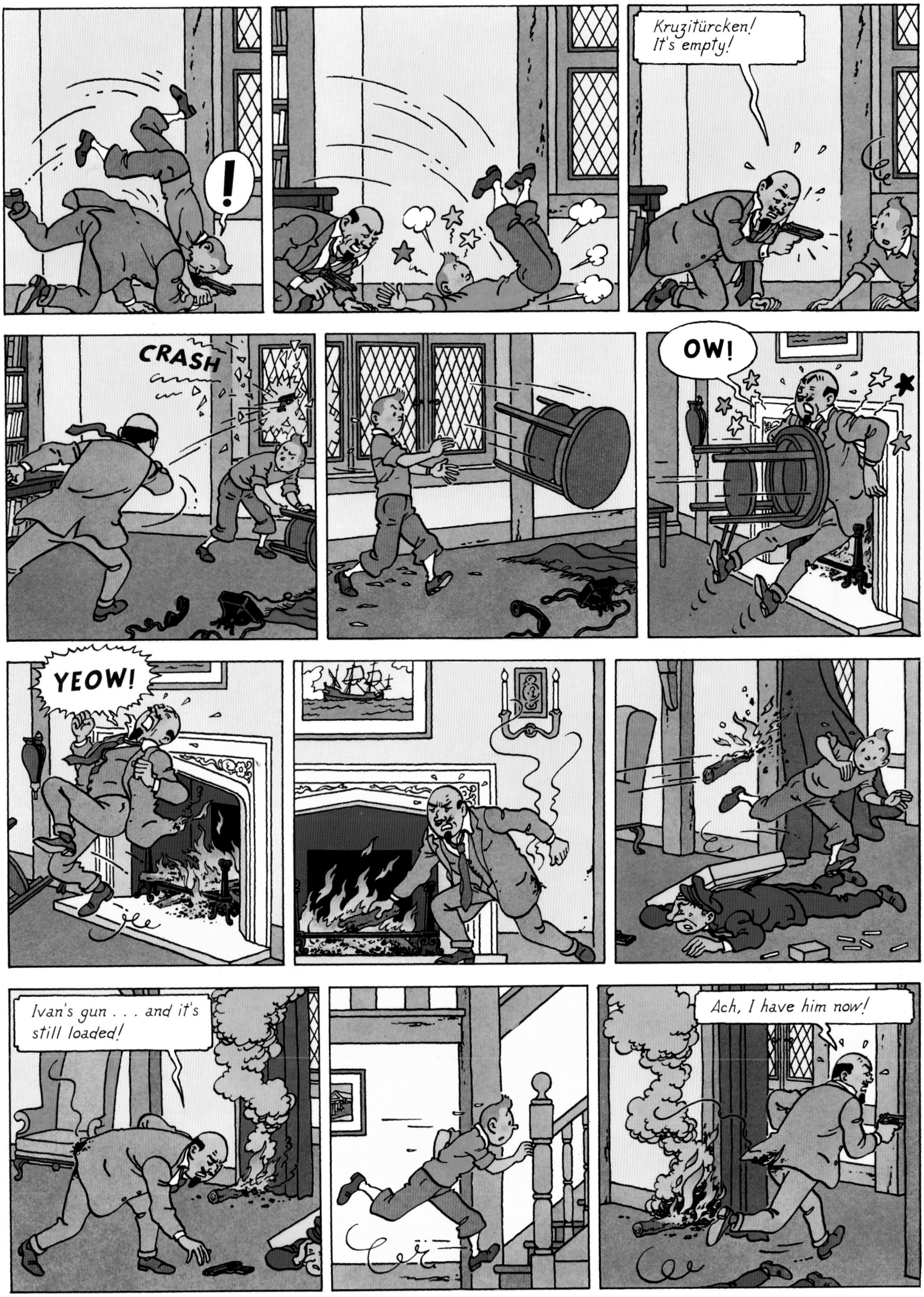

Kruzitürcken! It's empty!
CRASH
OW!
YEOW!
Ivan's gun . . . and it's still loaded!
Ach, I have him now!

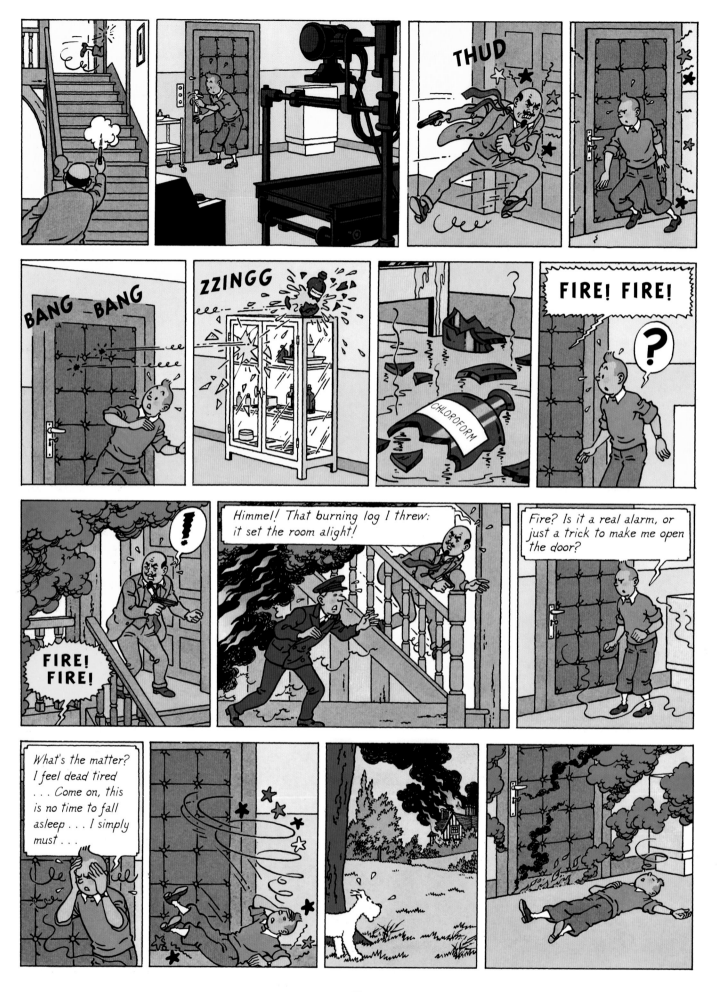

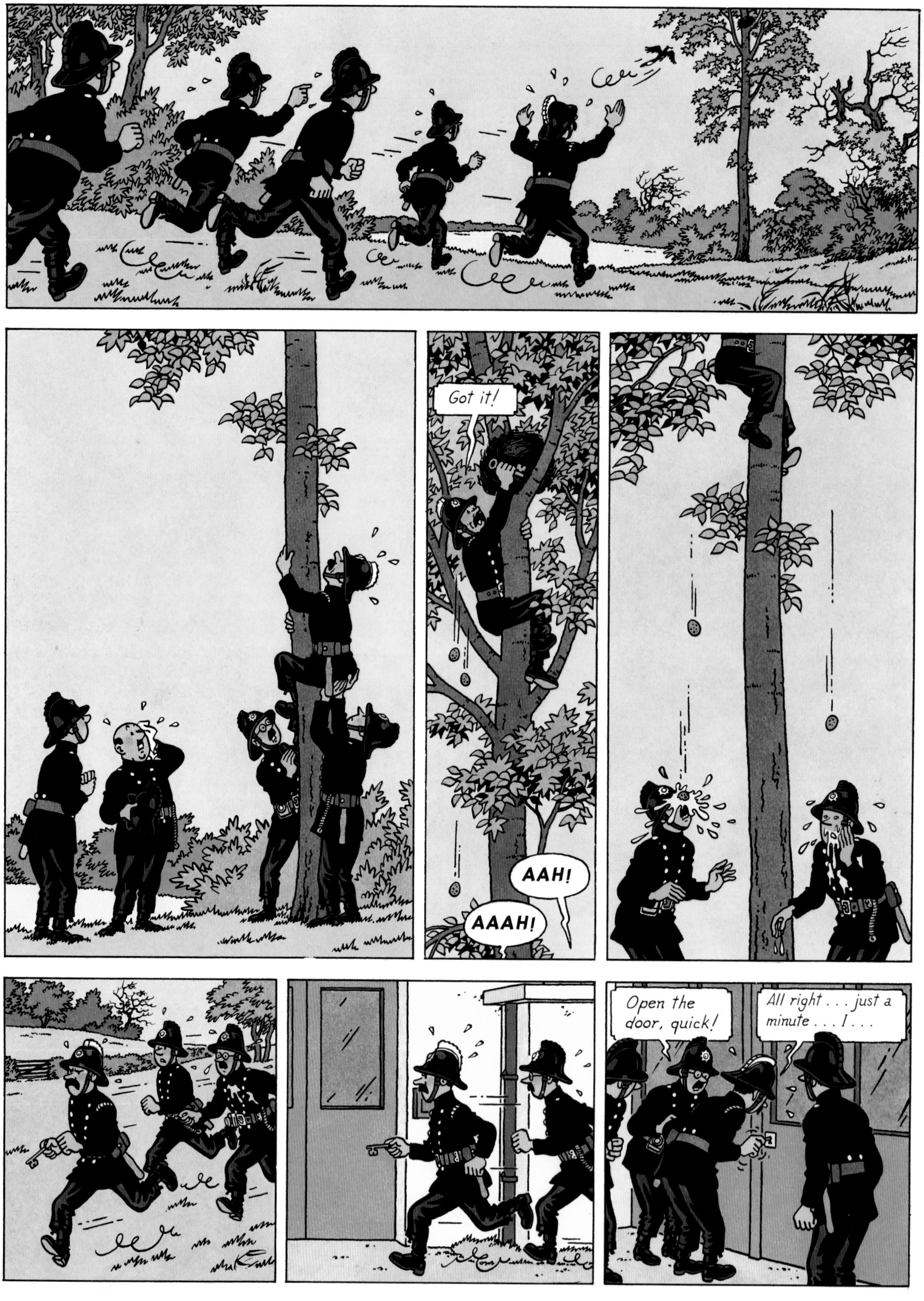
Got it!
AAH!
AAAH!
Open the door, quick!
All right . . . just a minute . . . I . . .

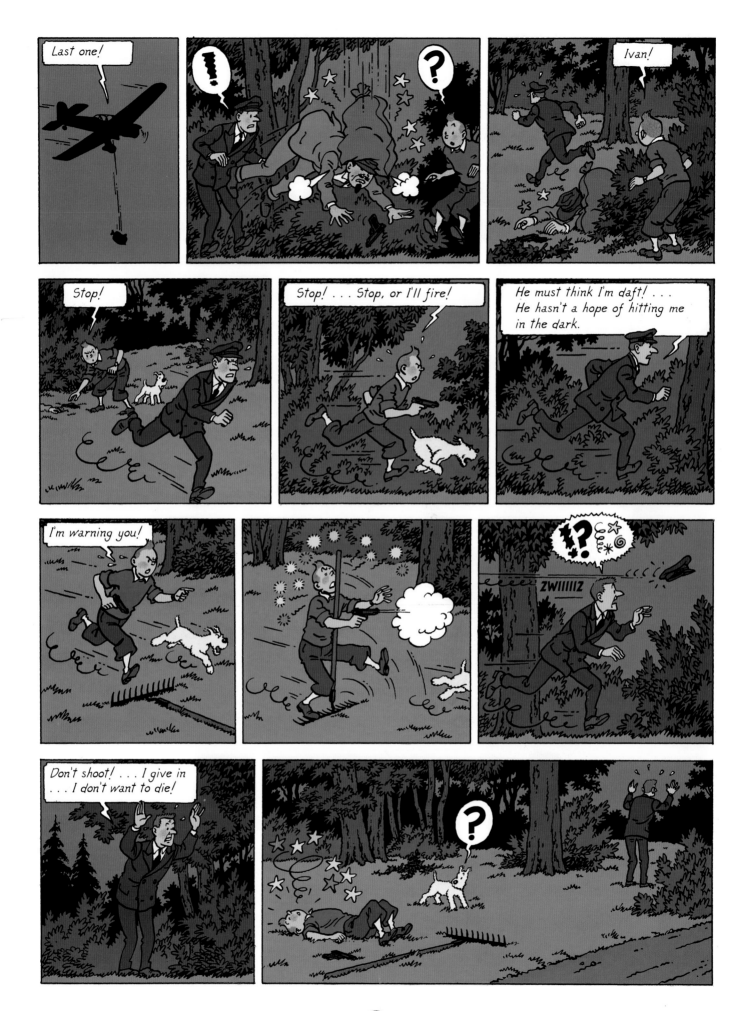

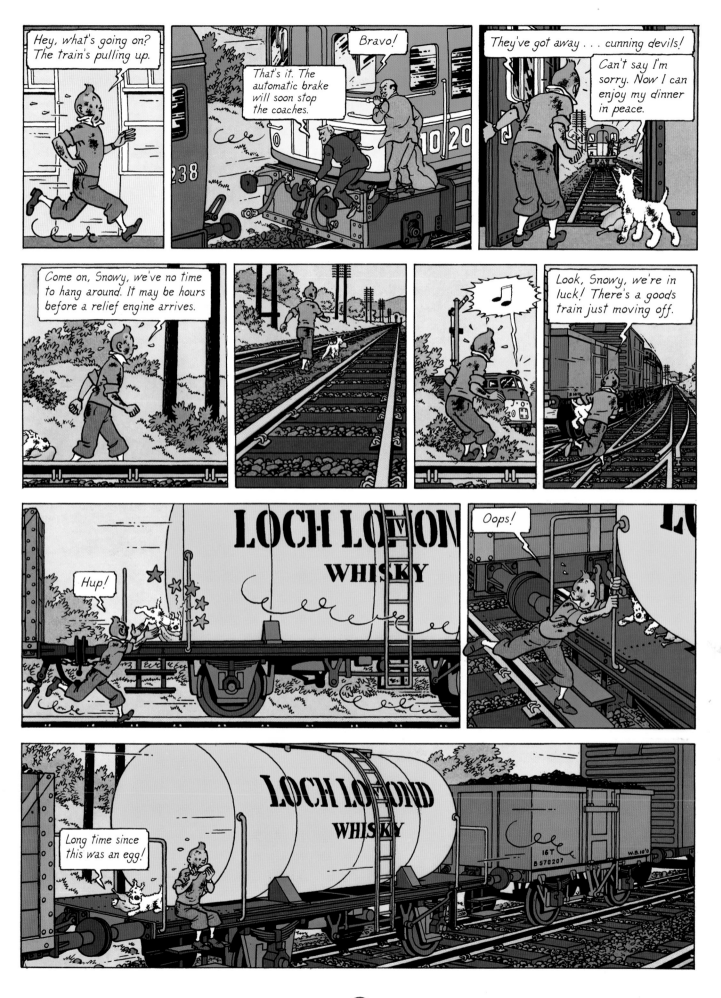

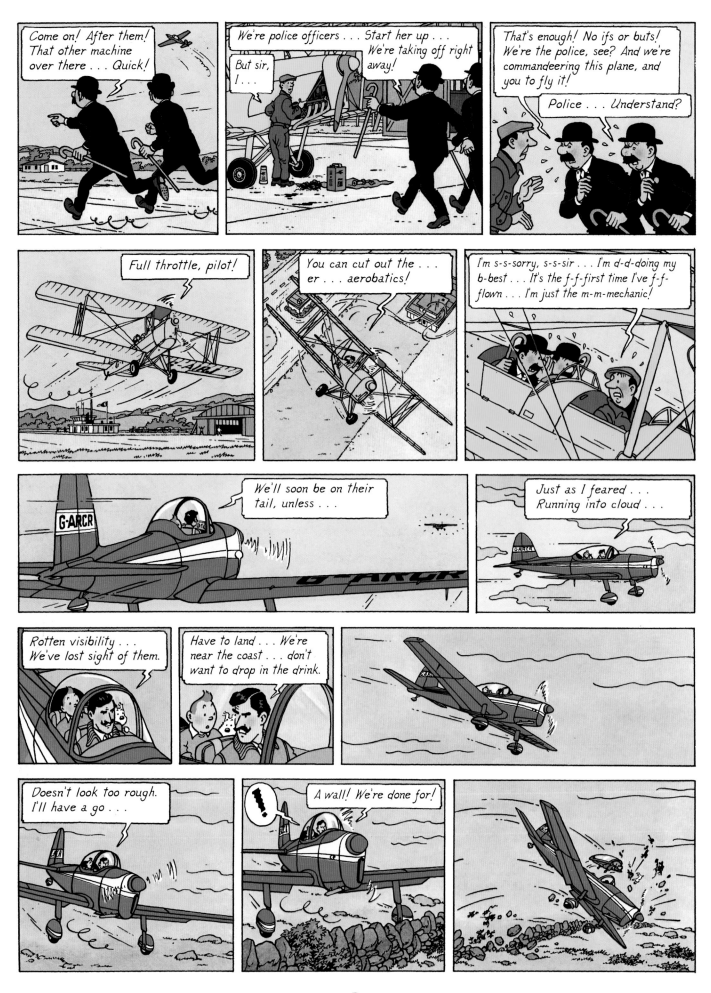

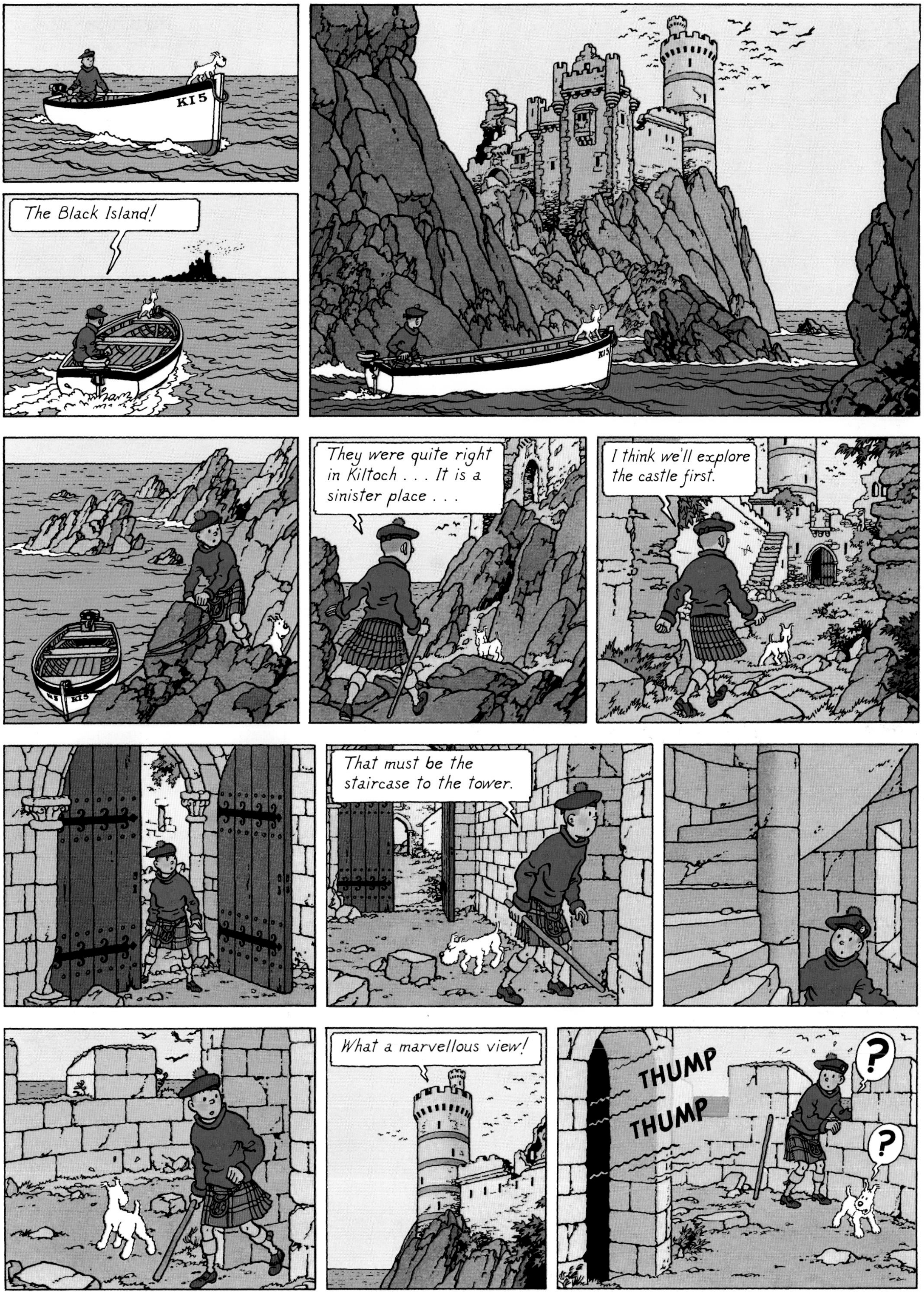
KI 5
The Black Island!
KI 5
They were quite right in Kiltoch . . . It is a sinister place . . .
I think we'll explore the castle first.
That must be the staircase to the tower.
What a marvellous view!
THUMP
THUMP
?
?

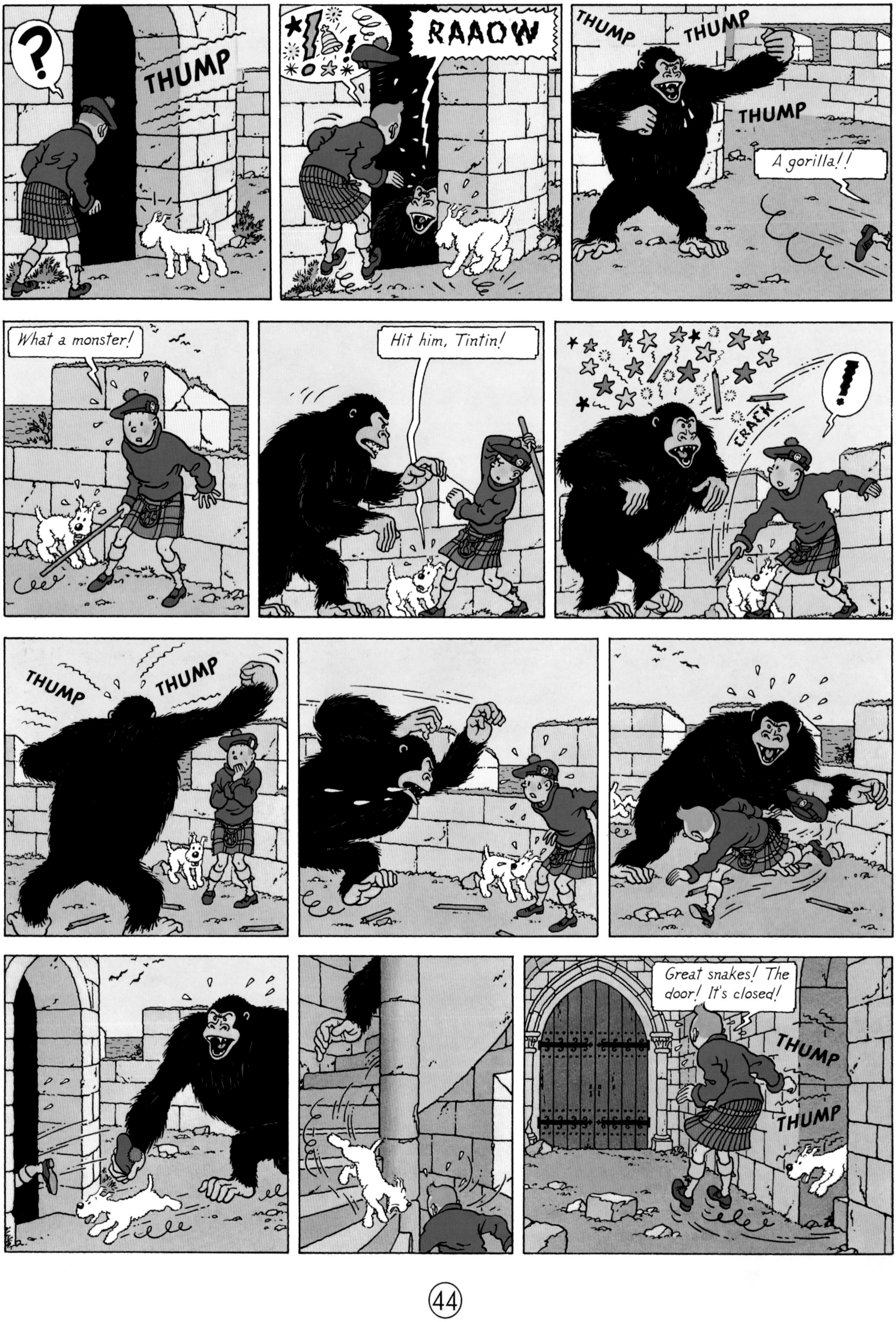
?
THUMP
RAAOW
THUMP
THUMP
THUMP
A gorilla!!
What a monster!
Hit him, Tintin!
CRACK
!
THUMP
THUMP
Great snakes! The door! It's closed!
THUMP
THUMP

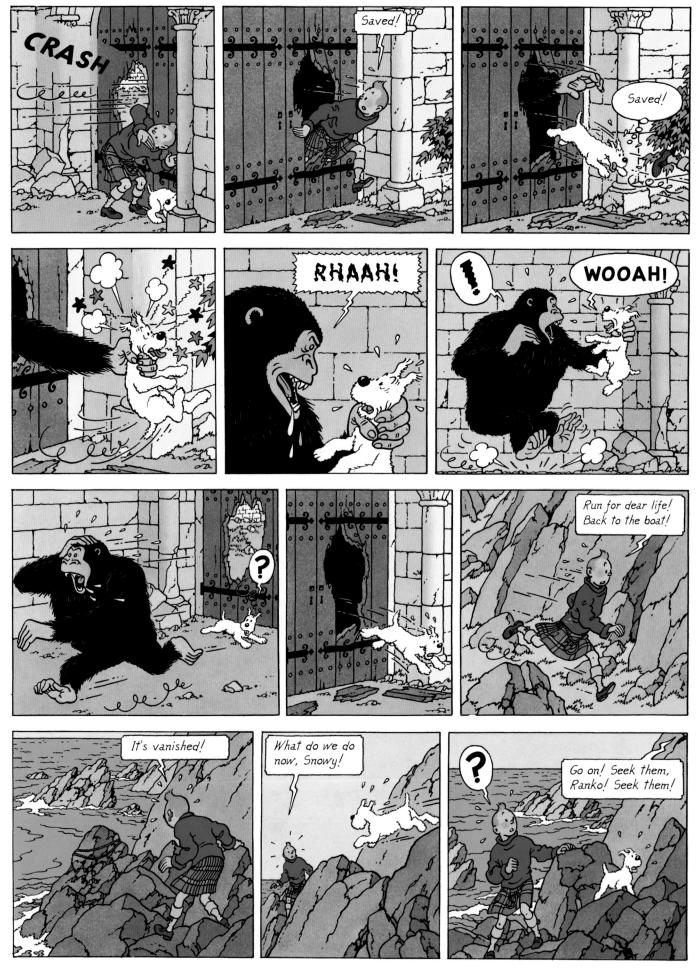

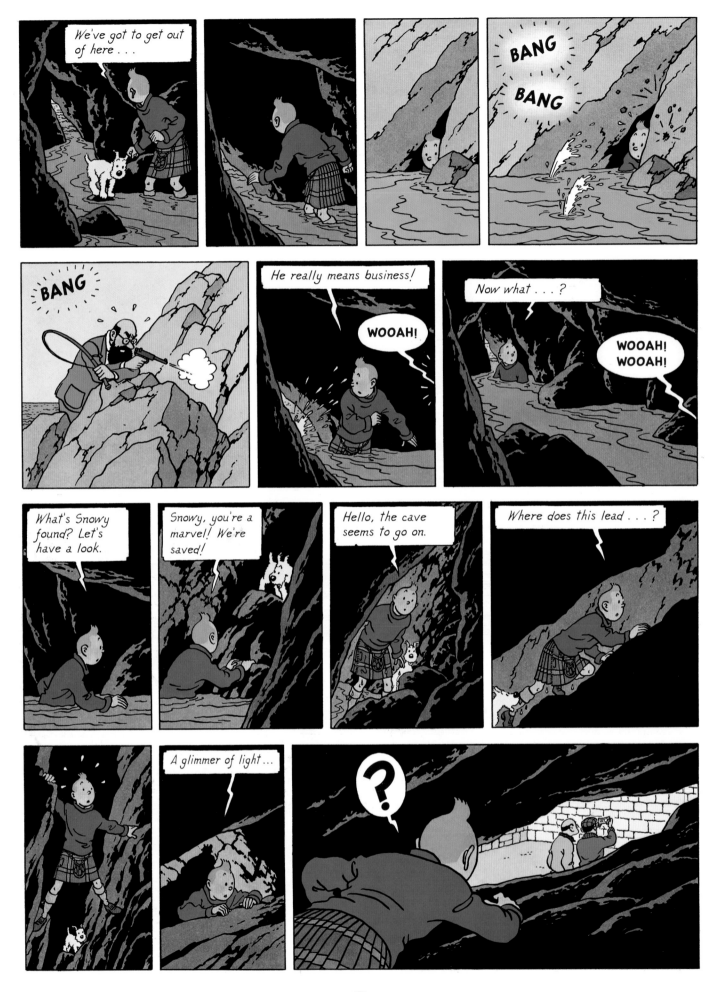

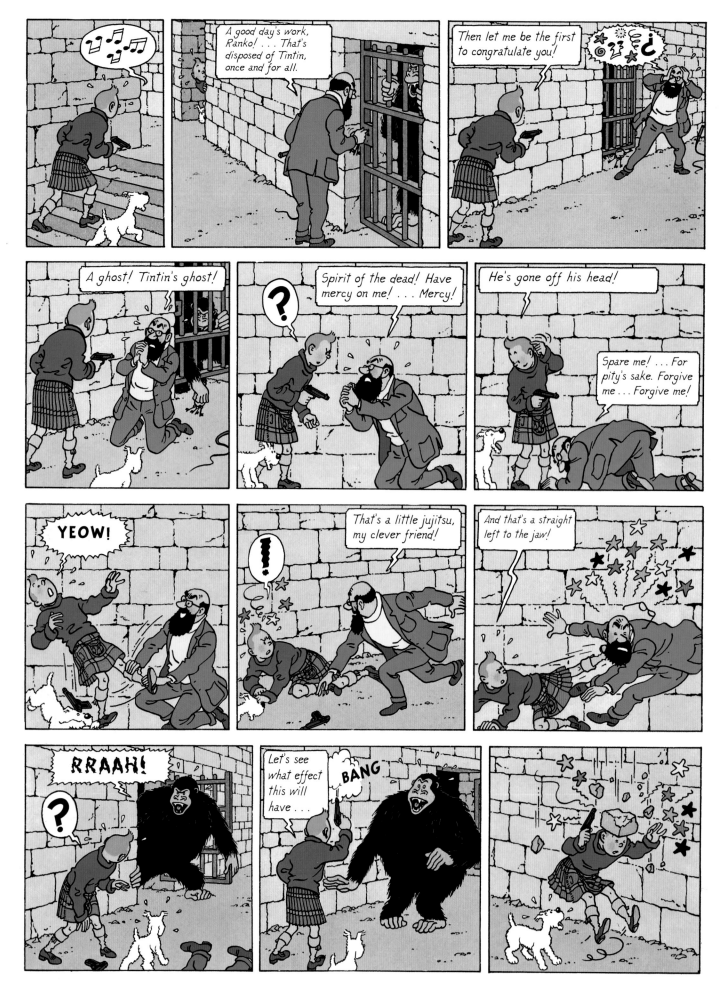

52